# Call Me
# Friday
# the Thirteenth

# Call Me Friday the Thirteenth

## BETTY BATES

DRAWINGS BY *Linda Strauss Edwards*

A YEARLING BOOK

Published by
Dell Publishing Co., Inc.
1 Dag Hammarskjold Plaza
New York, New York 10017

Yearling ® TM 913705, Dell Publishing Co., Inc.

ISBN: 0-440-40984-5.

Reprinted by arrangement with Holiday House
Printed in the United States of America
First Yearling printing—March 1985.

CW

*For* GERI, *with love*

# Contents

# Call Me
# Friday
# the Thirteenth

# 1.

# The Bump on My Forehead

"I ask you, Dad, was it fair for Ellen Englehart to smack me with her flashlight just because I upchucked on her mosquito netting?"

"You upchucked?"

"Yeah. Blueberry pie."

"Pretty messy stuff, Gussie."

"I didn't plan it like that. Anyway, I felt rotten. A person shouldn't hit a person when she's down, and I was really down."

"Really down, huh?"

"Well, I was down because I felt rotten. But in another way I was up, because my bunk was on top of Ellen's. I aimed at the floor, but her mosquito netting was in the way."

"Blueberry pie. Sticky stuff."

"Was it fair, Dad?" I asked, feeling the bump on my forehead that had turned a repulsive shade of purple.

He shrugged. "Maybe not."

"Dad, you know it wasn't fair."

"Blueberry pie, for pete's sake." He shook his head.

I didn't bother to tell him that Brenda Borenburg and I had stolen that pie from the kitchen of Camp Winnapoo for Girls and split it. So how come Brenda hadn't upchucked too?

And how come my dad didn't seem to care?

I've got this funny father who won't say more than five words at a time. A few minutes ago he'd shown up at Camp Winnapoo in the rain wearing his floppy porkpie hat, ready to drive me home. He helped me stash my wet sleeping bag and footlocker in the station wagon, stepping over puddles. It wasn't till he fitted his long legs into the driver's space, hunched himself over the wheel, and steered onto the gravel road that he finally spoke. "How'd you get that bump?" he asked in his low, rumbly voice.

But after I told him, all he did was shake his head and say, "Blueberry pie, for pete's sake!" Maybe if I'd gotten more sympathy from him then, I wouldn't have headed into such awful trouble later on.

My bump didn't hurt any more, because the bopping had happened night before last. I was still plenty sore at Ellen, though, and the soreness hurt. Still, when I got home, Mom would be sure to sympathize.

I leaned my head against the backrest, settling in, listening to the thud-thud of the windshield wipers. "We had a neat canoe trip. Went way up the river and camped overnight." Why should I mention that I had to scrub all the pots because I poured dirty dishwater on Brenda when we were on cleanup detail? "The mosquitoes weren't too bad," I said.

"That's nice." Dad turned onto the highway.

I thought about home, wondering how Mom was, and my nine-year-old brother Tomtom, and Figaro, the dog, who's exactly my age, which is ten-going-on-eleven. "How's everything at home?"

"Things are moving along. No problems."

That time he said six words, but the idea's the same. When I say my dad's funny, I don't mean he's funny ha-ha. I mean he's funny silent. I think he was once frightened by a tape recorder.

"I got my wood-carving certificate."

"Mm." He steered onto the approach to the thruway.

"Only got one check against me."

"Mm." He speeded onto the thruway.

"See, if you cut yourself, they put a check by your

name. If you get three checks, they won't let you near the sharp stuff."

"Mm." He passed a Mullins Moving van.

"I wouldn't even have had one check if that toad Gloria Guthrie hadn't hollered when the blood from my thumb squirted onto her elbow."

Dad took off his hat and scratched the bald spot over his forehead.

If spurting blood didn't get his attention, nothing would. In fact, nothing I said ever seemed to. I gave up and examined the bandage on my thumb. Anyway, Mom would be sure to pay attention when I told her about Ellen Englehart and Gloria Guthrie.

Camp Winnapoo is around seventy-five miles from home, but the heavy silence made it seem more like seventy-five hundred before we were back in Bramble City.

As Dad and I sloshed through the rain, hauling my gear into our little ranch house on Chokecherry Street, Mom followed our dog Figaro into the kitchen and scooped me into her arms, sleeping bag and all. "Oh, Gussie!" Her round eyes were dark and misty, like puddles. Finally she gave a little sniffle and straightened up. "How was it, honey? Did you have a good time? And what in the world is that thing on your forehead?"

"Seems there was some problem about blueberry pie," said Dad.

"Blueberry pie?"

"Well, see, I ate a tiny bit too much, and then it all came up, and Ellen hit me."

"But you don't get sick that easily. You must have eaten a whole lot more than you were supposed to. Gussie, did you and your friend Brenda get ahold of a whole pie somewhere?"

How come she always figures things out? I mean, she just knows things, as if she's got ESP or something.

"Um, well, there was a whole bunch of them just sitting there in the dining-hall kitchen, all by themselves with nobody around. And Brenda and I just happened to be going by on our way to the campfire sing, and, well, there they were."

"Really, Gussie, haven't you got even an ounce of self-control?"

"Ellen Englehart didn't have much self-control when she bopped me with her flashlight."

"On your forehead, I suppose."

I tried to explain, while Dad carried my footlocker into my bedroom, and Mom and I followed. Mom opened the footlocker and started to help me put things away. "I must say, Gussie, that anybody who

steals a blueberry pie deserves to get smacked."

Was she trying to hold back a smile?

"It was Brenda's fault too."

"All right. So you share the blame." She set my brush in the dresser drawer, and when she turned around the smile had busted out. "It is kind of funny, though." After a minute she straightened out her face. "Gussie, I'm sorry about the bump. Really, honey. But I just wish you'd stop and think sometimes before you get into these messes. And change those wet shoes and socks. Now."

While I was fishing in my footlocker for dry dirty socks, the phone rang, and Dad answered in the big bedroom. "Yes, she's here." He came back into my room and nodded at Mom. "It's for you, sweetheart. Sounds urgent."

Mom hurried into their room, next to mine. "Hello . . . Yes . . . Hospital? . . . Oh, no! . . . Oh, pooh! I'm so sorry. I'll come out there, of course. Thank you. Tell her I'll be there as soon as I can."

She wandered back into my room with her face all pale and shocked-looking, as if she'd just bumped into something very sharp. "It's Bo. The hospital called to say she had a fall and broke her hip. I really do have to go, Paul."

Bo is Mom's mother, who lives hundreds of miles away in California in one of those towns with a Spanish name. I was really sorry she'd busted her hip. On the other hand, I was going to be stuck in the house with a dad who seldom speaks and Tomtom, who never shuts up, and Figaro, who's always hungry.

Crum! How long does it take to recover from a broken hip?

# 2.

# Quit Worrying, Mom

Out in the driveway, Karen and I were jumping rope, while Figaro watched us, with his bloodhound eyes swooping up and down. Karen's my best friend. When she bobs around she's like some bouncing ball, and she can do loads more jumps than I can.

"So did your dad find anyone to take Mrs. Perkins's place?" she asked, breathing hard.

"Nope."

Mrs. Perkins is the sitter Mom got to take care of us while she was gone. Only Mrs. Perkins had come down with awful asthma, and Dad was trying to get someone else, and Mom, out in California, was frantic.

My aunt Kit had asked us all to come and stay in

her big old house on Fern Avenue, provided Tomtom and I wouldn't track in mud or set off illegally imported firecrackers. I was kind of disappointed when Dad turned her down. There's lots of action over there with my cousins in and out. Dad doesn't go much for action, though. So my two aunts, who are married to Dad's two brothers, kept sending over soupy casseroles. Was I ever sick of soupy casseroles and canned tuna and baked beans!

"How come you hardly ever trip on that jump rope?" I asked Karen.

"It's simple, Gussie. All you need to do is take it easy." She twisted the rope to form a circle and jumped through it.

"I can't take it easy."

"You do when you're playing first base."

"Softball's different. It's back and forth and sideways. This is up and down. You've got to be a human yo-yo."

She started jumping double time. I could have killed her.

The phone rang in the kitchen. I hoofed it into the house and waded through the swimming and softball junk on the kitchen floor to catch the phone on the ninety-seventh ring. "Hello."

"Well, hello!" It was Mom. "I almost hung up," she said. "How's everybody, Gussie honey?"

"Not bad. Tomtom swallowed too much water when the kids from Camp Joy went swimming at the city pool yesterday because he opened his mouth to laugh at Jonathan for doing a bellyflop. It was okay, though. The lifeguard gave him artificial respiration."

"Artificial respiration?"

"Only as a precaution."

"Are you sure he's all right?" She sounded the least bit hysterical.

"Sure, Mom. Right now he's probably still over at Jonathan's." Jonathan's his best friend, who lives in the next block.

"But he ought to be home. It's nearly six your time."

"He'll be home when he gets hungry. Supply and demand."

"I wish you'd try to keep better track of him, Gussie dear. He's still awfully young."

Was he ever!

"So what about you?" she asked. "Is your forehead okay?"

I'd nearly forgotten about the bump, even though she'd asked about it whenever she called. Anyway, the purple blotch had disappeared. I felt my forehead, which was absolutely smooth. "It's a little better. In fact, Karen and I were out jumping rope. That's why it took me a while to get here."

I couldn't see any point in wrecking her day by mentioning Mr. Zerbel's fence. Mr. Zerbel lives in the ancient brick house on our corner. He's as old as a caveman and built like one—not exactly the kind of person you'd want to meet on an empty stomach. I think he's a little psycho, because he's got this big stone on his front lawn with a sign beside it that says HERE LIES A TRESPASSER.

That morning Karen and I hadn't intended to scrape paint off his back fence when we had the accident while dueling with sticks while riding our bikes no-handed. Besides, we went to a whole lot of trouble to touch up the scratches after the caveman threatened to complain to our families.

"Gussie, what about the laundry and the meals? Did Dad find a sitter yet?"

"Uh-uh. We're doing great, Mom, honestly," I said, ignoring the kitchen floor.

"How's Dad?" asked Mom. "Is he home yet?"

"Nope. He's been working late a lot."

She sighed. "I know." Dad's got his own one-man accounting business, with Platner Plastics as his biggest client. So whenever they have a problem with what Dad calls their cash-flow situation, he knocks himself out. He hadn't even had time to work in his vegetable garden in the backyard past the maple tree, which was overgrown like some jungle. But I knew he'd call Mom that evening. They were always talking on the phone.

"You coming home soon, Mom?"

"Honey, it's going to be a while. Bo's staying in the hospital about another week, and they haven't got enough help there, so I'll have to stick with her. Then I'll take care of her at home while she recovers. She's awfully brave, but oh dear, I do miss you!"

"Sure. We, um, miss you too, Mom." There seemed to be a frog in my throat.

She just had to come back before school started. My homeroom teacher was due to be Mr. Sherer the Terror, who had once caught me removing the light bulbs from the principal's office during a fire drill and had been grinding his gravelly teeth at me ever since. You're supposed to be outside during a fire drill, so why wasn't he? I could never survive Mr. Sherer and his teeth without Mom to fortify my strength.

"Give my love to Tomtom," said Mom. "And Dad." Her voice cracked.

I hate it when people's voices crack. " 'Bye," I said quickly. "And quit worrying, Mom. We're okay."

When Dad walked in the door around six-thirty, Tomtom wasn't home yet, Figaro was slopping his dinner all over the clothes on the floor, and I was opening our very last can of baked beans.

# 3.

# Burned Hamburgers

"Where's Tomtom?" asked Dad.

"That's what Mom wanted to know."

"Mom? Did she call?"

"Mm-hm. Bo's going to take forever to get well."

He nodded slowly. He looked tired, and his shoulders were all saggy. He must miss her a lot, maybe almost as much as I did.

Tomtom banged in the door in his bathing suit and smudgy Camp Joy T-shirt, the one he'd been wearing all week. "Wow, am I starved! What're we having, Gussie?"

So I'd been appointed chef.

"What's it to you, merman? You never bother to help."

"I'll do the cleanup."

"Sure. When you do the cleanup you leave all the mangy pans sitting around soaking. Think they're going to get up and walk away?"

He stuck out his tongue.

"Go put some dry clothes on, Tomtom," said Dad.

"Come on, Dad. Nobody ever catches cold in the summer." He dropped his towel on the floor and opened the cookie canister, which I happened to know was empty.

"Pick up your towel," I snarled. "And the rest of your stuff."

"Half of it's yours."

"Well, pick up your half."

Dad covered his eyes with his hand and sighed. He opened the flatware drawer and lifted some out. Three forks, three knives, three spoons.

Tomtom was gone, and the towel was still there. I was finding out what Mom goes through.

Dad set the flatware on the kitchen table, stooped over to pick the wet towel off the floor, and disappeared into the hall.

Just as the beans boiled over, the phone rang. I grabbed the saucepan and answered it.

"Hi ho there, Gussie."

"Hello, Aunt Kit." Aunt Kit is married to my

dad's older brother, Uncle Mac. Her name's actually Katherine, but in our family everyone's got some nickname. Everybody except my dad, who's just plain Paul.

"Gussie dear," said Aunt Kit, "how are you all?"

"We're great. Just great."

"I'm going to send my Emmeline over there Monday to clean up for you. She's got the day free."

This was the third time she'd offered to send Emmeline. The last person I wanted in the house at eight in the morning was Emmeline, with her mops and dustrags and cheery personality. Thank goodness Dad felt the same way.

"Please don't bother, Aunt Kit. We're fine, honestly."

"Well, if you're sure."

"I'm positive."

"Gussie, can I trust you to take a message?"

"Sure, Aunt Kit. Have I ever failed you?"

She gave me that bouncy laugh of hers. She didn't even mention last Christmas, when I'd forgotten to tell Mom we were supposed to bring forks.

The saucepan was heavy in my hand, but I didn't dare set it on the Formica, because I'd once dumped a hot frying pan there, and Mom had to have all the counters redone.

Aunt Kit went on. "Big family picnic for Uncle Mac's birthday. A week from Sunday at four."

"Great. What'll we bring?"

"Now don't you bother about that. Not with your mother gone."

"It's okay, Aunt Kit. Look, we've got piles of rolls in the freezer. We'll bring them."

"Gussie, I really don't think—"

"It's all settled. I'll even bring my Frisbee."

"Well, all right, but keep it away from the potato salad this time, will you, dear? And, Gussie, are you writing this down so you'll remember?"

I plunked the saucepan on the floor, opened a drawer, and reached for the pad and pencil Mom always keeps next to the phone directory. "Of course I am, Aunt Kit. How could you doubt me?"

"I never did, honey. See you soon then. Hi ho to all of you."

Aunt Kit's got that sort of Scottish highland swing to her voice, as if she's calling the sheep from the hills. Maybe I'd hate that sort of thing if I hadn't been surrounded by it all my life, but since I'm used to it, it's like music to me.

The burn on the kitchen floor from the saucepan would probably wear off. I shifted my sweat shirt over to cover it up, and at dinner nobody noticed. Tomtom had on shorts with wet spots where the water from his bathing suit was soaking through. Well, he had put on dry clothes.

"We need groceries," said Dad.

"Right," said Tomtom. "We're out of cookies."

"So you two need to make a list and go to the store tomorrow after Tomtom's day camp."

I chewed on a hot bean. "You heard him, Tomtom. Karen and I will be at softball practice. You can go."

"Can't. Got a date with Forrest, the lifeguard. He's going to show me the backstroke."

"So cancel the date."

"Will not. Who says you have to stay at softball practice all afternoon?"

"We've got a game Saturday. Anyway, who says you've got to go swimming after day camp? You've just about turned into a fish, hanging out at that pool all the time."

Dad cleared his throat. "Ran into Joe Zerbel downtown today."

Crum! The caveman must have told him about that back fence. I swallowed very hard. I didn't know what to expect, because Mom always handles the discipline, and she can get pretty tough.

"He said you and Karen didn't do a bad job of touching up his fence." His eyebrows and his nose and mouth and ears were in the same positions they're usually in. There was no expression. He never

gets excited. All he does is talk once in a while in that rumbly voice of his. So how was I supposed to figure out if he was mad or not? He's been around me all my life, and I still couldn't tell.

"Big picnic," I said quickly. "For Uncle Mac's birthday. Week from Sunday at four. We're taking rolls and the Frisbee." I remembered everything without looking at my note. Crum! I hadn't needed to burn the floor after all.

While Dad went to call Mom, Tomtom actually did do the cleanup, leaving the saucepan soaking in the sink. Dad changed into slacks and slapped on his porkpie hat and drifted out to do yard work for a change. While he was mowing the lawn, the phone rang. "Hi there, Gussie." It was Uncle Mac. "Everything all right? Anything we can do?"

"No thanks, Uncle Mac. We're fine."

"Well, if there's ever anything, we're only too willing. Listen, Gussie, is your dad around?"

"He's mowing the lawn. I'll get him."

"No, never mind. Just give him a message. I'm going over to Gravel City tomorrow, and would you tell him not to do anything with those figures I gave him till I get back? You got that, Gussie?"

"Sure, Uncle Mac. Have a great time in Gravel City."

Dad does the accounts for Uncle Mac and Uncle

Stew's glass manufacturing company, and Uncle Mac's always going off to Gravel City on business and leaving messages.

All this money talk reminded me of my allowance. Mom gives it to me on Fridays, so it was almost two weeks overdue.

I had a little money left from my store deposit at camp, but not much, so I traipsed outside. Dad was now ripping weeds out of his bean patch. I told him what Uncle Mac had said and added, "Say, Dad, um, how about my allowance?"

He looked up. "Allowance?"

"You know. Money."

"Money." He screwed up his eyes as if I'd just invented some new word. "Gussie, my wallet's in my regular pants. Catch me when I come in, okay?"

"Sure. Hey, Dad—" I was planning to ask him to come to our game on Saturday, but he'd already turned back to the weeds. Anyway, he'd probably be busy working.

He must have slipped back into the house later on, but I missed him, maybe because I was in my room, wrapped up in *Judge Benjamin: Superdog,* a book about a St. Bernard who helped his family get through a tornado.

The next morning I was dumping eggshells into the sink when Karen poked her head in the kitchen door and got a close look at the junk on the floor. "Eee-uck! It's worse than ever. Looks like some kind of stew."

I guess I'd gotten immune to the sight, but now I could see what she meant. She helped me push the clothes into a corner. No point in overdoing the neatness.

After we'd burned a batch of brownies and tried on all my blouses and analyzed all the girls on our softball team, it was time to slap together sugar-and-cinnamon sandwiches for lunch.

We were on our way to softball practice when we just barely cut across the caveman's corner. I mean, neither of us took more than three steps on his dumb old lawn. Well, maybe five or six. All of a sudden there was a terrible roar from his upstairs window. "Watch that grass!" There he was, leaning out of the window without even a shirt on, with hair covering his chest like some shag rug.

"Let's pretend we didn't understand him," said Karen.

So we smiled and waved as if we were movie stars meeting our public, while he kept snarling like some volcano ready to erupt. Finally he banged the window shut. Karen and I took off, giggling, and she ended up with the hiccups.

Softball practice was over in time for Karen and

me to buzz down to State Street and stop in at Cactus Corner, which is the lounge at the Bramble City Motor Inn. The place has got this enormous, prickly cactus plant right in the middle that looks like something off the moon, and there are pictures all over the walls of cowboys and cactus. During the cocktail hour there's a whole table of snacks, and there's no sign anywhere that says you have to buy a drink to sample the spread. Besides, the cocktail waitress, whose name is Gina, has got a smile as big as the entire West. So once in a while we duck in and mix with the crowd and fill paper plates with snacks. I particularly like the meatballs, which taste like small, gloppy hamburgers. We sneak the food through the swinging doors and outside, while Gina pretends she doesn't see.

Lately I'd been noticing Mr. Thistle, the inn manager, giving us the eye as we passed his office off the lobby, but I figured that was only because Rupert "The Brain" Thistle is in my class at school and may possibly have a crush on me.

Naturally I was late getting home. When I walked in, Dad was in the kitchen reaching cans out of a brown paper bag.

I'd forgotten about the food.

"Crum! I forgot about the food."

"I know," said Dad, hauling out the ground beef.

I felt so guilty I offered to cook hamburgers. While Dad was in the garden picking salad greens, Tomtom showed up.

"Wash your hands, Tomtom, and get some potato chips into a bowl."

"Who was your slave last year?"

"The Wizard of Oz. Come on, Tomtom, just do it."

While he was digging into the potato chip box, it slid off the counter. He stepped into the middle of it, and pieces of potato chips squished out onto the floor. It was all I could do not to grab the frying pan with the hamburgers in it and bean him on that scruffy head of his.

We were picking up the pieces when I smelled something burning. I turned around, to see black smoke rising from the frying pan and Dad standing in the doorway. "Pretty black smoke, huh, Gussie?"

Was he smiling? I couldn't quite tell. And if he was smiling, was he smiling *at* me or *with* me? I never know.

So for dinner we had burned hamburgers and pieces of potato chips, plus salad. All through the meal Tomtom and I argued about whether it's more revolting to eat black hamburgers or fractured potato chips, while Dad sat between us with his head turning back and forth, like somebody watching a tennis match.

After dinner I remembered my allowance. When I found Dad, he was in the big bedroom calling Mom. "Don't worry, sweetheart," he was saying, "everything's fine."

Sure. Everything was fine.

I staggered to my room, clicked on the radio, and lost myself in the thumping of the music.

# 4.

# The MacIvers

Uncle Mac and Aunt Kit and their three children live with Grandma MacIver in the original family house on Fern Avenue, that runs along the hill. Every year we celebrate special days with them and Dad's younger brother, Uncle Stew, and his family, plus all the out-of-town relatives who can make it. It's always a madhouse, like behind the scenes before a school play. If you hadn't known my family for ages, you'd need one of those electronic gadgets to keep everybody straight.

This time there must have been over thirty of us, uncles, aunts, grandparents, and cousins, and half of them were asking Dad how we were getting along and offering to come and cut the grass. Uncle Stew and his family wanted to take Tomtom and me off Dad's hands, which was very self-sacrificing of them. But I was relieved when Dad turned them down. Those kids are okay, but big doses of them are hard on the stomach since all four of them are little and very fizzy, like Uncle Stew.

I spent my time with my cousin Samuel, who's my age. He belongs to Aunt Kit and Uncle Mac, and he gets called Mule, which is the perfect name for him on account of his big ears. Mule's okay because he doesn't pretend he hates girls.

After a while we got tired of tossing the Frisbee with Tomtom and the other younger kids. We milled around through the smell of bug spray in the big yard between the house and the tables set up back toward the woods. The adults drank silly things like Scotch-on-the-rocks, and we kids drank soft drinks. The adults' laughter got louder with each drink. I missed Mom's laugh. It sort of sparkles like a Roman candle, and she's always in the middle of things.

Mule and I edged over to the bar table, where Uncle Mac was joking with Uncle Stew and a couple of cousins from out of town. While we were pouring ourselves the last of the root beer, Uncle Mac turned around and said, "Gussie, we certainly do miss that mother of yours," and banged me on the back. Uncle

Mac's pretty big, and when he bangs you on the back you notice it.

Mule nudged me. "Get a load of Grandma. She looks as if she's escaping from a burning building."

There she was, clomping down the back steps in hair clips, a yellow dress, and her clattery slippers. Grandma's five thousand years old, with a little round face that's dried up like a raisin, and she's losing her marbles.

I snickered. I felt kind of guilty, though. I mean, after all, she didn't plan to lose her marbles.

My cousin Corky, Mule's sister, who's tall and blond and probably the most popular girl in this year's Bramble City High senior class, drifted toward Grandma, smiling that smile of hers that's like caramel. Her lips moved, as if maybe she was asking Grandma if she could help. "My pearls, Corky," yowled Grandma. "Somebody stole my pearls again."

She never can find her pearls, and she's always sure they've been stolen, and she always thinks everybody else is as deaf as she is.

Dad was winding his way toward Grandma. He laid his hand on her wrist and leaned way over and spoke in her ear, and she calmed down. After a while she nodded and went back into the house with him.

People were gathering at the long table where the food had been set out. Roast beef, ham, potato salad, cole slaw, pickles, and all the rest. Everyone was taking filled plates to the long eating table.

While Mule and I were piling our plates a foot high, I noticed Dad helping Grandma down the back steps. Now she was wearing sandals. The curlers were out of her white hair, and it was combed so it wasn't flying all over the place, and thank goodness she had her pearls on.

After we'd gathered at the table, we didn't sit down. This was on account of what I call the MacIver mumbo jumbo. I mean, we go off into all kinds of toasts and speeches, depending on the occasion. This family stuff might seem goofy to a lot of people, but I was brought up on it.

So when everybody was quiet, Uncle Stew waved his paper cup in the air and called out, "A birthday toast to Mac, chief of the Bramble City MacIver clan through the good and the bad, the high and the low. Here's hoping he lives forever, so many happy returns, Mac old boy."

"Hear, hear!" "To our leader!" "Here's to Mac!"

Uncle Mac beamed, slipped his arm around Aunt Kit, and said, "And here's to Kit, the wife who puts up with all my foolishness, Lord love her."

Aunt Kit's blue eyes shone while we all yelled

"That's right!" or "To Kit!" or "Hurray for Kit!"

Dad was the only MacIver brother who hadn't spoken. He only stood there towering over Grandma and wearing a faint, faraway smile. So what? I was used to that.

As we sat down and dug in, I felt a sort of glow about being a member of a family that sticks together.

Maybe it was all that root beer.

Mule's two sisters sat across from us. If you didn't know, you'd never believe they were related, with Corky peaches and cream like Aunt Kit, and Pug dark and husky like her dad, Uncle Mac. Mule is somewhere in between. He's dirty blond, with glasses. Pug has the MacIver brains, but she got short-changed on looks. Somewhere along the line somebody must have paired off with a bulldog. She even talks the way a dog would talk, in a sort of woof.

"What happened to Grandma?" asked Corky. "I was afraid to look."

"Nothing," Mule told her. "Uncle Paul rescued her before most people noticed the weird getup."

I made a grab for the salt. "He even fixed her hair. I never knew my dad could do hairdos."

Mule laughed, and I joined in.

Pug leaned forward. "What on earth are you children talking about?"

When I explained, she said, "I think you're very

cruel. Senility is not something to be made fun of."

Pug was nineteen going on ninety. Just because she was in college, she didn't need to act so superior. Still, it made me sad about Grandma. At family parties when Mule and I were little, she used to read *The Three Bears* and *Snow White* to us, and the way she'd wiggle her voice around when she said "Mirror, mirror on the wall" used to crack us up.

Pug shoved her pigtail back over her shoulder. "Gussie, I wish you'd see that Tomtom changes T-shirts once in a while. He's setting a poor example at day camp."

She's activities counselor at Camp Joy, and naturally she expects Tomtom to be perfect.

"Look at it this way, Pug. Think how much cleaner the other kids feel by comparison."

"Gussie, really! Somebody ought to do some laundry at your place once in a while. Is Mrs. Perkins still in the hospital?"

"Yup. Now the doctors think she's got some kind of pneumonia. It's a shame."

"It certainly is. What about your meals? Bet you're starving. And I can imagine the mess."

"Actually we're tearing up the place."

"I thought so."

She's got no sense of humor.

"It's a pigsty," I went on. "Food slopped all over

the kitchen floor. Orange juice, cornflakes, fried eggs. Whole meals."

Corky giggled.

Pug gave her the bulldog stare. While Corky winked at Mule, who was choking on a pickle, Pug turned to me. "I'm going to start stopping off every day after day camp to make sure you don't starve and to keep your place in order."

Crum! The MacIvers are supposed to stick together, but this was too much. "Listen, Pug, I was kidding. It's neat. It's like a hospital. Antiseptic. Not a germ in sight."

Pug's lips were a straight line from cheek to cheek. "We'll see."

There was no use arguing. When she makes up her mind, dynamite won't budge her. My only hope was that she'd forget.

Except that Pug never forgets.

# 5.

# Good-bye Forever

The next afternoon Karen and I rode our bikes downtown to stock up on shampoo and other useless junk, and I spent the last of my money. We stopped off in the library to pick up books for the summer reading program.

Miss Concannon, the children's librarian, calls it the zoo program. She gave us bookmarks with animal pictures on them. For every three books we read she sticks a star on our bookmark next to a lion, a bird, a seal, or whatever. There's a poster on the wall behind her desk, with a picture-diagram of a zoo. There's a path leading to the lion house, the aviary, seal island, all that stuff, to correspond with the animals on our bookmarks. At the end of the path is the popcorn machine, where she letters in your name when you've finished the whole program. Big deal. I wouldn't bother with it except I've got this terrible weakness for getting my name in public places. One time Sherer the Terror caught me writing it in the wet concrete for the new sidewalk in front of school.

So now I'd made it as far as the elephant house, and Karen was at seal island. After we'd picked up more books, and after Miss Concannon had kicked us out of the library for dropping stones from the plant pot into the card catalog, it was time to head for Cactus Corner.

Gina was on her way to a table with a tray of beers. I expected her to flash us her western smile, but she frowned instead. What had got into her? The men at the table looked like Platner Plastics workers, so naturally they knew her, and every one of them had to make some gross comment about her blue, blue eyes or her dimples. So Karen and I joined the snack line, trying to look like somebody's children. When we were as far as the cheese dip, Gina edged up to us. "You girls better watch it. Mr. Thistle doesn't want you coming here."

"Golly, Gina," I said, "you'd think he'd be glad to have us. We swell the crowd. We keep the chef busy."

"I don't know about that, but I do know this food

is for customers. Mr. Thistle says his cash-flow situation is getting worse and worse, and you're helping to block the flow, so you've got to cut it out. Didn't he tell you when you went past his office?"

"We didn't see him."

"Then I'm supposed to tell you."

Crum! Cash-flow situations were ruining my life.

Karen tipped her head back and gave Gina her soulful look. "So it's good-bye forever?"

"It's good-bye forever. You'd better hustle yourselves out of here."

We left the motor inn through the side door to the parking lot so we wouldn't pass Mr. Thistle's office, and wrapped ourselves around the food. Somehow it didn't taste the same.

At Karen's house, she said, "See you tomorrow, Gussie."

"Right."

Since the caveman was sitting on his front porch, I was careful not to cut across the lawn. In fact, I even waved at him. Mom always says it never hurts to be friendly.

Mondays never seem to go right somehow. On top of everything else, Pug was there when I got home. With those snacks inside me, I wasn't exactly starving, but the smell of baking chicken made me wish I hadn't overdone it on the miniature sausages. The kitchen was picked up and wiped clean. I'd never be able to find my Camp Winnapoo sweat shirt or my orange-and-green striped socks.

Pug was at the counter cutting the ends off of string beans she must have picked from Dad's garden. Her pigtail hung down the back of her Camp Joy T-shirt, and the muscles of her legs stuck out from under her shorts. "Hi, Gussie," she said. "You hungry?"

"Sure I'm hungry." Baked chicken will hook me every time.

"Clean up your room then. You get your dinner when that place is neat, and no hiding stuff in the closet or under the bed." She must have learned all the angles from Mule. Those poor kids at Camp Joy! It ought to be called Camp Misery.

"Golly, Pug, my room's already neat."

"Neat like a tornado. I checked when I dumped your things in there because I wasn't about to go wading around this kitchen. I'll check again before dinner."

"Um, look, Pug, I've got a book to finish for the library reading program. I'll clean up my room tomorrow."

She turned toward me with the knife in her hand. "I said *before* dinner, Gussie."

"Pug, listen—"

"Strawberry shortcake for dessert."

The combination of the strawberry shortcake and the knife in her hand convinced me.

Half an hour later, each of my drawers was a disaster from all the junk I'd crammed into them, and Pug had dinner ready. When Dad wandered in the kitchen door, he seemed even droopier than usual, as if a small truck had run over him and bent him at the shoulders. Pug must have noticed too. "Something on your mind, Uncle Paul?"

"Well, the Platner Plastics situation—" He blinked at her. "You staying for dinner?"

She slapped the chicken dish onto the table. "I will if you like. I'll call Mom and let her know."

Now why did Dad have to go and ask that question?

Luckily for me, Pug decided to pick on Tomtom while we were eating. "Tomtom, must you stuff chicken into your mouth?"

"Sure. Tastes sho good."

"Must you talk with your mouth full?"

He swallowed. "Nope. I can talk both ways. See?"

She looked at the ceiling.

Then she looked at the floor. "What's your mother going to say about that?" she asked, pointing to the burned spot.

She always was a troublemaker.

"Say about what?" asked Dad.

"That spot, Uncle Paul. I'm sure it wasn't there before."

He stared, in a sort of daze. I could picture those Platner Plastics account figures zooming around inside his head. "I don't think she'd worry, Pug," he said.

Whew!

After dinner I caught him on his way to call Mom. "Dad, do we have to have Pug around?"

"Pug? Why not?"

"She's a menace, Dad. She even made me clean up my room."

"Not a bad idea, Gussie girl."

"It looks like some prison cell."

By this time he was in the bedroom pushing buttons on the phone, and I'd forgotten again to ask for my allowance, and he'd be in there for hours, and Mom didn't seem any closer to coming home, and school was only a month off.

After that it got to be routine for Pug to stay for dinner. It was an awful strain getting ordered around like some army private and keeping my stuff in drawers and never being able to find anything. Still, sometime during that week the weeds disappeared from Dad's garden, and we were finally getting decent meals, so I guess Mom's right when she says that every thorn has its rose.

On Saturday morning, Pug went shopping and stocked up the fridge and freezer. "I found more chicken in your freezer. Bet you didn't even know you had it." She shook her pigtail. "Bet you never even looked in that corner."

The trouble with Pug is that she's always right.

I left her plunking a box of dog food down on the counter. The phone rang, and I answered it in Mom and Dad's bedroom.

"Gussie honey, how are you?"

"I'm okay, Mom."

"That's nice."

"Only I need my allowance."

"Your allowance? Hasn't your father given it to you?"

"Nope. Could you remind him sometime when you're talking to him?"

"Gussie, I really don't understand why you can't do that yourself."

"Never mind, Mom, I'll work it out."

"Your forehead must be all right by now."

"My forehead? Oh, yeah. It's improved a little."

"I'm glad. Is Dad there?"

"He's working."

"Pooh! Can't you get him to slow down? If he kills himself doing those accounts, Platner Plastics will be even worse off."

"I know, Mom. Hey, how's Bo doing?"

"I thought you'd never ask. She's out of the hospital. I'm calling from her place."

"Then you'll be home soon, huh?"

"Honey, I need to stay for a while. I have to find someone to help Bo out. I'll get home as soon as I can."

"Before school starts?"

"I really can't say, dear."

I thought of Sherer the Terror and felt slightly nauseous.

"Shall I give Bo your love?" asked Mom.

"Oh, sure." I don't know Bo very well. She comes for Christmas once in a while, and she's tall and skinny and stooped, and she pats me on the head a lot, and right now I wish she'd get the heck well again.

"Dad tells me Pug's looking after you."

"Mm-hm."

"Bet you're all having fun together."

There was the sound of our fridge door being slammed shut.

"Um-hum."

"Could I talk to Tomtom?"

"I'll go wake him up."

"Oh, no. If he's still asleep, don't bother him, poor little thing."

Poor little thing, my foot!

At our softball game that afternoon, Karen and I each made a run. Karen may be little, but she's got power.

After the game she and I decided to celebrate our team's win, which naturally meant food. "I'm starving," said Karen. "Got any cash?"

"Absolute zilch. How much you got?"

She dug into her shorts pocket and hauled out a quarter and some pennies. You can't get hamburgers or pizzas at Ozzie's for thirty-two cents. It was four o'clock, so dinner time was way off. We could raid the Pratts' fridge, but Karen's mom always hangs around and asks questions. Going to my place, with Pug there, was obviously impossible.

Karen raised her eyebrows. I shrugged.

We pointed our bikes toward the motor inn.

What else can you do when you're broke and hungry and homeless?

# 6.

# My Dad Won't Like It

Streaking past the hardware store on our bikes, we nearly knocked down an elderly couple who were coming out with a pitchfork. "Well, really!" said the elderly lady.

"Sorry!" I yelled over my shoulder, barely missing a mother pushing her baby in a stroller.

We locked our bikes next to a grease spot in the motor inn parking lot and slipped in the side entrance to avoid Mr. Thistle again. Mr. Thistle knows my dad from the Chamber of Commerce, and unfortunately he probably remembers me from the annual father-daughter dinner, when I won my Samson indestructible watch as a door prize.

Just our luck. When we were nearly down the first

hall, somebody yelled from behind us. "If it isn't Gussie MacIver." I'd have known that squeaky voice anywhere. It was Rupert Thistle, looking like a blown-up paper bag. I wished he'd take a long walk off a short pier.

He inspected us from under those toothpick bangs of his. "Good afternoon, you two. You're tracking grease in."

Sure enough, there were black patches on the carpet all the way down the hall to the door. Karen gulped. "Sorry."

Seemed as if we were doing nothing but apologize to people.

Rupert narrowed his bubble eyes. "Don't tell me you're crazy enough to come back to Cactus Corner. You know how my dad feels about that."

"We're looking for a friend," I said.

"Sure," said Karen. "We're looking for a friend."

Well, Gina's a friend.

Rupert stuck out his chin. "I can't imagine you have a friend anywhere in this motor inn."

"Well, we do," said Karen, tugging my shirttail. "Come on, Gussie."

We hightailed it down the hall, with Rupert calling after us "My dad won't like it."

As we turned the corner toward Cactus Corner, we peeked back over our shoulders. Rupert was watching us with a very thoughtful expression. "Hey, Gussie," said Karen, "he's watching us."

"So what? We could be heading for the pool. We could be going almost anywhere."

"Sure, Gussie, sure."

Cactus Corner was pretty dead. It dawned on me that very few people would stay at a motor inn in Bramble City on a Saturday night. Always before we'd been there on week nights, and we could lose ourselves among the traveling salesmen and workers from Platner Plastics. But now there were only three men who badly needed shaves draped over the bar staring into their glasses, and two couples ogling each other at tables. Gina was chatting with the bartender. When she saw us, she gave us a disgusted look. "Girls, we said good-bye forever. Remember?"

"Sure, Gina," I said, "but we rode our bikes for miles to get here, and we're starving. Completely hollow. Carved out."

While I talked, Karen had edged toward the food table. All they had were a few slices of cheese and some crackers. Probably their regular Saturday spread. "Puh-lease, Gina," said Karen. "Just a cracker and a piece of cheese. You're a good person, Gina, a really kind lady."

The men at the bar had quit staring at their drinks and were watching, kind of half smiling. Gina sighed.

"All right. One piece of cheese and one cracker apiece, and then I don't want to see you again till you're of age, you hear?"

The cheese was slightly stale, the cracker crumbled in my hand, and when Karen and I were ready to leave, our stomachs were still growling. "Thanks for nothing much, Gina," I said.

"You're welcome," she said, smiling.

Saturday afternoon is not the time to find sustenance at Cactus Corner.

We detoured to the ladies' room off the lobby, where we each picked a stall, locked the inside lock, and crawled out under the door.

That should fix the Bramble City Motor Inn.

We watched the ladies' room from down the hall. The next person who went in was a woman you could've sawed in half and made two of. She'd never make it under one of those doors.

After a minute she came roaring out, as if somebody had set off dynamite, and headed for Mr. Thistle's office.

Karen and I took off down the hall. As we turned the corner, I glanced back. There was Mr. Thistle, stepping out of his office. He squinted at us. Karen and I kept running. In the parking lot we were panting. "Gussie, he saw us!"

"He couldn't tell who we were. He's nearsighted,

and he didn't have his glasses on."

"How do you know he's nearsighted?"

"From the way he squints. Nobody squints like that unless they're nearsighted."

"Sure, Gussie."

When I got home, Pug was setting the table for dinner. "Mr. Thistle called," she said.

Crum!

"Mr. Thistle? Who's he?"

"You know perfectly well who he is. He thought I was your mother. He said you've been causing problems at the motor inn."

"Me?"

"You and Karen."

"Me and Karen?"

"He asked me for your friend's phone number. Gussie, were you two at the motor inn today?"

"Well, um—"

"Were you, Gussie?"

"We might've passed through on our way somewhere."

She'd never tell Dad. She wouldn't.

"I'm going to tell your father."

She would.

"Pug, we didn't do anything."

She turned back to the table and slapped down a napkin. "Your dad will be the judge of that."

I knew better than to argue with her. Once she makes up her mind, she digs in so you can't budge her. I stuck my tongue out at her pigtail, dashed into Dad and Mom's room, and called Karen. "Did Mr. Thistle call your mom?"

"Uh-huh. Dad's home, and she told him."

"She did?"

"And I'm grounded for ten whole days."

"Karen, that's awful."

"Wisdom through suffering, Dad says."

"I'll come see you."

"You can't. Nobody's allowed."

"Oh."

"Especially you."

Mr. and Mrs. Pratt have never liked me. They probably think I lead Karen astray, which is like thinking the bears got Goldilocks into trouble.

"What happened to you, Gussie?"

"Dad's at the office, but Pug's going to tell him, the fink!"

"What'll he do?"

"I don't know. That's the trouble. I just don't know."

# 7.

# Squishy Shoes

Dad speared a hunk of the salmon Uncle Stew had brought over from his fishing trip. "Let's not have any more of that, Gussie," he said.

I mean, that's all he said.

I mean, honestly!

I would have felt better if he'd bawled me out. At least he'd have been paying some real attention to me. But now I felt let down, the way you'd feel if you stepped on the bottom step and it wasn't there to support you.

While we were scraping our plates after dinner, Dad said, "Your mother's got some outside help for Bo."

54

"Hey, neat," said Tomtom. "That means she'll be back here soon, huh?"

"Not all that soon. She'll stay with her for a while and make sure things are going smoothly. Hard to find just the right person sometimes. We found that out ourselves."

After he'd left to call Mom, Pug said, "I cannot understand your father, I simply cannot. Why he didn't punish you, Gussie, is way beyond me."

Tomtom began scraping his food onto my plate. "I'll bet he's still worried about the Platner accounts, and about Mom too. Otherwise he'd have really given it to you."

"Tomtom, will you get your stinking fish bones off of my plate? You're always—"

Pug cut in. "Those fish bones do not stink, Gussie. And even if your father is worried, the least, the very least he could have done was send you to your room. Why didn't he?"

A little of Pug goes a long way, and a lot of Pug goes much too far.

Later on, I found Dad in the living room hunched over his paper. "Did Mom say when she'll be home?"

He gave me a tired look. "Nope. Look, Gussie, we have to make up our minds that it's going to be a while."

Crum!

So now what? Should I thank him for not sending me to my room, which Mom would have done without even blinking? Should I try to explain my side of the situation, maybe talk the whole thing over with him? After all, I had a cash-flow problem of my own, which is what caused the whole mess in the first place. I needed my allowance.

As a substitute for Mom, he'd struck out.

He turned to the financial section, shoved his glasses up on his nose, and frowned. I took a deep breath.

The phone rang.

I ducked into Dad and Mom's bedroom and answered.

"What did he do to you, Gussie?" asked Karen.

"Nothing. Absolute zero. Goose egg."

"Terrific."

"Yeah. Terrific."

"I'm very jealous, Gussie."

"Uh-huh. Listen, Karen, I'll call you every day. I'll tell you all the news. I'll bring you library books and leave them inside your front door."

Life wouldn't be the same without Karen.

After I hung up, I couldn't find Dad. Tomtom was watching a car chase on TV. "Where's Dad?" I asked.

"He went to the company party at Aunt Kit and Uncle Mac's."

Crum! Trying to corner Dad is like some little kid trying to corner Santa Claus.

Softball practice was all wrong that week. Skinny Diane Dunn, who took over Karen's shortstop spot, can barely catch a ball, much less throw it. We were playing against our second team subs, and Diane kept tossing it toward my ankles when I was expected to put someone out at first, and their runners kept marching around the bases like some parade. Finally I resorted to accidentally getting in the way of the runners whenever they got near first base.

At our game on Saturday, I did the same thing to Beth Balenger from the Bluebird team, who fell when she dodged me. She picked herself up with a trickle of blood running down her leg, burst into tears, and took off for home, while Meg Melvin, our pitcher with the exploding tonsils, called out, "Really, Gussie! Did you have to use unfair tactics?" when it was obvious that Diane Dunn's tactics had been unfair to me.

Naturally we lost the game.

When I told Karen about it on the phone, she said, "You shouldn't have done that, Gussie."

"You're probably right, but you know how it is nowadays. All the emphasis is on winning."

"That's no excuse."

"Hey, how come you're so preachy all of a sudden?"

"Who knows? Maybe I'm just plain bored. I think I'm going out of my gourd, Gussie."

"I wouldn't be surprised," I said helpfully. "What'd you do today?"

"Watched TV. Fought with Mom. Read. Watched more TV. Wrote in my diary. Fought with Mom again. Read some more. Those library books for the reading program you dropped off, I've read them all twice, and I should be at the monkey house."

"That figures."

"Gussie, are you implying—"

"Listen, I'll get you more books. I'm going to the library before softball practice on Monday."

"Okay. I'll leave the ones I've finished on the hall table with my card."

"Karen, I can't wait till you get sprung on Wednesday. With Diane Dunn out of there, we might even win our next game."

"Remember, Gussie, it's not whether you win or lose, but how you play the game."

"Sure, Karen."

Close confinement had definitely affected her mind.

On Monday morning I slept till around ten. The

sky was dark. If it rained, our one o'clock practice would be called off, and when I rode my bike to Karen's and the library, I'd have to go to the trouble of stuffing my books into a plastic bag.

Also, I'd planned to get my allowance from Dad for sure this morning, five weeks' worth, but he was bound to be at the office.

By the time I got dressed and crammed clothes into drawers, and collected my books from under my covers and off the bathroom floor, and made my bed, it was almost ten-thirty. Pug, who was vacuuming the living room, raised her eyebrows. "Are you expecting breakfast or lunch?" she asked, shoving Dad's easy chair to one side and digging the vacuum into the carpet.

"Don't worry. I'll find something to eat. How come you're not at Camp Joy?"

"Camp Joy ended on Friday."

Crum! Didn't she have anyplace else to go?

She snapped off the vacuum. "I'll get you something. I'd just as soon you didn't mess up my kitchen."

So it was her kitchen now.

"Pug, I can get my own food."

"I said I'll do it, Gussie."

"You will not." I stamped toward the kitchen.

We collided in the doorway. Pug clenched her

teeth. "Don't be so stubborn, Gussie. You are honestly the most pigheaded—"

"You're the one who's pigheaded. You came here and took over without even being asked. You're trying to push me around and run my life and treat me like some kind of baby."

"Well, of all the ungrateful—I'm calling your dad."

When she says she's going to do something, she means it. So let her. I was out the kitchen door with my books and rain hat. I raced into the garage, threw the books into my bike basket, and took off for Karen's. By this time it was drizzling. I plowed ahead. I was so mad I even cut across the caveman's lawn. He wasn't on his porch, probably on account of the rain, but as I hit the sidewalk I heard his door open. "I'm calling your father, Miss MacIver."

With all those phone calls, Dad wasn't going to be able to put much of a stop to the problems of Platner Plastics.

The farther I went the harder it rained. By the time I got to Karen's, my T-shirt and shorts were sticking to my skin. The front door was closed on account of the rain, so I had to ring the bell. Mrs. Pratt showed up at the door dressed in her blue-green-yellow-orange-and-purple smock. She had Karen's books in a plastic bag, and while I stood there getting dumped on she asked me why I wasn't wearing a raincoat and how Bo was getting along and when Mom would be coming back. Obviously she didn't care if I drowned.

While this was going on, Karen was sneaking down the stairs, and while I was saying that Bo needed an awful lot of care, Karen was wiggling her nose like some rabbit and stretching her mouth wide with her thumbs and rolling her eyes in their sockets, and it was all I could do to keep a straight face. Finally I lost control and burst out laughing, and Mrs. Pratt said "Really, Gussie, you don't need to be rude" and shut the door in my face.

Everything happens to me. They should have named me Friday the Thirteenth.

Since Mrs. Pratt hadn't given me the books yet, I rang the doorbell again, but she didn't open the door, probably since she must have discovered Karen behind her, because there was an awful argument going on inside.

My T-shirt and shorts were sopping. Water was dripping off my nose.

I knocked again, louder.

Finally the door opened. Mrs. Pratt handed me the plastic bag without a word and closed the door.

I sat on the front steps and emptied the water out of my gym shoes.

If I were Karen I would pack my clothes and my

diary and join some sort of religious sect.

Naturally my own library books were just about curling up from all the rain. I dumped the plastic bag on top of them, hoping to prevent more damage, and raced for downtown, splashing through puddles.

Sometimes life seems to have lots more puddles than sunshine.

At the library, I squished into the children's room in my wet shoes and set all the books on the counter in front of Miss Concannon. She slipped my books out from under the plastic bag and blinked her mascaraed eyelashes. "Really, Gussie! Just look at these books."

"Well, see, Miss Concannon, when I left the house it wasn't raining."

She drummed her orange fingernails on the counter. "But you should have known. I'm afraid I'm going to have to charge you for the damage."

"But, Miss Concannon, I haven't got any money."

"Then I'll have to take your library card away. I'll call and let your mother know, and when you bring the money in you'll get the card back."

If she called, Pug would answer the phone.

"My mother's out of town, Miss Concannon."

"Oh? Then I'll call your dad at his office."

How did she know about my dad's office? She must be one of those people he does income tax for.

"You don't need to call, Miss Concannon. I'll be sure to remember. I sure will."

"You surely will, Gussie. Surely is an adverb modifying the verb will."

"Sure, Miss Concannon."

She frowned through her mascara, glanced at her list of phone numbers, and picked up the phone.

Oh, no! First Pug, then the caveman, and now Miss Concannon.

I didn't want to hear. I headed for the girls' bathroom to wring out my hair.

# 8.

# Food

So now I had the entire day to kill. Practice would definitely be called off, and I wasn't about to go home till dinner time, and I couldn't drop in on Meg Melvin, my second best friend, because I was mad at her for yelling at me during the game, and my aunts' houses are miles away, and I didn't have money to spend the afternoon at the movies. I squished back into the children's room, collected my last couple of books for the book program, and settled down with my wet shorts sticking to the chair. Luckily Miss Concannon was busy with other people. Still, I caught her giving me the old bullet eye now and then. She probably wondered if I'd suddenly decided to move to the library.

I was careful not to do anything to upset Miss Concannon. If she kicked me out this time, I'd have nowhere to go. I even sat through her story hour for small children without plugging my ears when she read the book about the talking motorcycle, or giggling when she knocked over her chair while imitating Miss Muffet.

Actually Miss Concannon is not a bad person behind her mascara. I know Karen and I are always giving her a hard time, but somehow when I'm with Karen I can't seem to help myself. When you put us two together, it's like matches and fireworks.

By the time my Samson indestructible watch said three-fifteen, my stomach was churning like Mom's food mixer. I mean, I hadn't eaten one thing all day, not even a peanut.

I'd finished the first book, about a boy who entered a fantasy world through the bathtub drain, when Rupert Thistle waddled in. "Well, if it isn't Gussie Mac-Iver!"

Rupert Thistle may be brilliant, but he's not very original.

"Hello, Rupert."

"Shh!" hissed Miss Concannon.

Rupert shuffled to the counter to talk with her about his books, and then he plodded over and plunked himself into the chair next to mine. "Well, if it isn't—"

"That's right," I whispered.

"How are you doing on the reading program?" He sort of wheezes when he talks, like when you let the air out of a balloon.

"I'll be at the popcorn stand if I can just manage to finish this book." I opened the second book and read the description on the inside jacket. The book was about a girl who planted zinnias which came up as talking trolls.

"I'm all done," said Rupert.

"That's nice."

"I'm reading extra books now."

"Mm."

"When you're an only child, you get lonely."

"Mm."

"And you read a lot."

"Rupert, I really would like to read this book."

"Sometimes, when I get desperate, I even read comic books."

Rupert Thistle reading comic books? "Comic books?"

He wriggled his rear end into his chair and leaned forward, with his face a sort of weird yellowish pink. I felt like throwing up.

He cleared his throat like a frog with a bad cold. "Well, there's *Z-Men,* and there's *Moro the Magnificent,* and there's *Dr. Weird,* which is a new one. It's about an old man who flies to another planet in his wheelchair and becomes youthful and strong again."

"But, Rupert, you can't fly to another planet in a wheelchair. I never heard such a bunch of baloney."

"Gussie!" Miss Concannon was giving me her barracuda look.

"Actually," whispered Rupert, "I don't think it's so great either. It's not true science fiction."

"It certainly isn't," I whispered back. I opened my book again and began to read.

"Where's Karen?" asked Rupert.

"She's home. Rupert, I really would like to—"

"What's she doing at home? She's always with you."

"Well, she's not now."

"You're like the headlights on a car. Whenever I see one of you, I see the other, usually at the motel."

He would bring up the motel. It was hardly fair of him. "Rupert, will you please—"

"She sick or something?"

"No, Rupert, she is not sick. She's merely home."

"You mad at each other?"

"No, we are not mad at each other, but I will be very mad at you if you don't quit—"

"Gussie MacIver, you're going to have to leave the library." It was Miss Concannon, of course, with that look of hers. My voice must have been rising. People were staring.

"But, Miss Concannon, I wasn't the one—"

"She wasn't the one," said Rupert, wheezing.

"She was the one who was talking loudly, Rupert. She was disturbing people who want to read." Miss Concannon tapped her fingernails again. "All right, Gussie, I'm waiting."

"I'm sorry, Gussie," said Rupert, drooping. "I'm always messing things up."

I let out my breath in a long, long sigh and unstuck my shorts from the chair. " 'Bye, Rupert," I said between my teeth, dropping my book onto the chair.

Loneliness does terrible things to people.

So there I was, out in the street in the rain again. I didn't have the book about the talking trolls. I didn't even have books for Karen. She wouldn't have anything to do except watch TV and write in her diary and fight with her meddling blue-green-yellow-orange-and-purple mother. She'd hate me.

And all this was happening to me on an empty stomach.

At a time like this, who wouldn't think of Cactus Corner?

Actually it made a whole lot of sense, my heading

there. Rupert wouldn't be around to warn his dad, and by this time the place would be jammed with people coming off the day shift at Platner. Gina would be charging around with drinks, and all I had to do was stay out of her line of fire. I could snatch all sorts of munchies in thirty seconds flat, enough so I could feed myself on the stairway by the side door and have some left to take to Karen to make up for not bringing her books.

At the side door of the inn, I emptied my gym shoes again and snuck down the hall toward Cactus Corner with water dripping from my shorts. In one of the housekeeping rooms, two maids were yammering. In a bedroom with the door open, a man, stripped to the waist, was doing push-ups.

There was so much racket coming from Cactus Corner it had to be bedlam in there, thank goodness. I ducked through the swinging doors behind two men in sport shirts and slacks. The bartender was swamped with customers, and Gina was standing by a table near the far corner waiting to take orders from a group of men and women. She looked vaguely in my direction, but the dreamy look on her face didn't change. I should have plenty of time.

There was a line at the snack table. I tried hiding behind the man at the end of the line with DIRTY DEEDS DONE DIRT CHEAP on his T-shirt. He was skinny, but he was all I had.

By the time I made it to the snack table, Gina was through taking the order and headed toward the bar, not looking my way. I grabbed a paper plate and a bunch of napkins, keeping my head down in case she changed direction. If she caught a glimpse of me, she might think I was the daughter of the man who did dirty deeds.

All through the line I kept my chin against my neck, grabbing bacon wraparounds and cheese crackers, and going heavy on the meatballs. A lavender skirt and red spike-heeled shoes were in back of me. Some combination! Thank goodness I wasn't pretending to be that person's daughter.

I didn't raise my head. I kept it down to the very end, even when I swerved around toward the door and got bumped into by some plaid slacks over brown-and-white shoes. "Excuse me," I mumbled, and took off past table legs, nylon stockings, and pigeon-toed shoes.

Outside the swinging doors, I nearly ran into some gray pants with creases like knives. I swung to the right. The pants swung the same way. I swung to the left. The pants swung too.

It was then that I looked up into the dark, horn-rimmed glasses of Mr. Thistle.

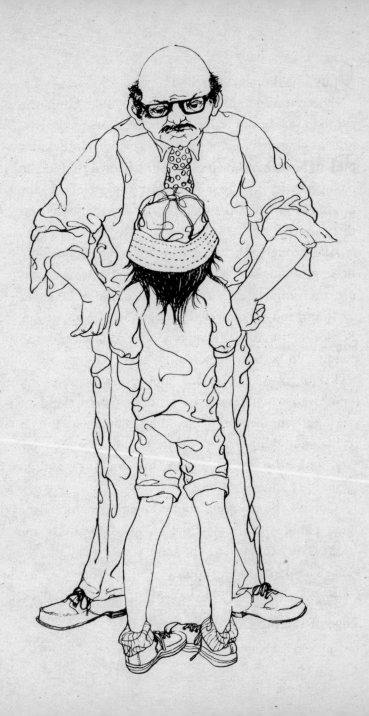

# 9.

# Phone Call Number Four

Somebody had betrayed me. Was it Gina? But she hadn't even smiled at me, or frowned either. The bartender? He was so busy he didn't have time to look up. Then who?

Rupert. He must have followed me out of the library. He'd probably snuck in and told his dad, and right now he must be around some corner, smirking. How could I ever have imagined he had a crush on me?

Yes, the traitor was definitely Rupert.

"We'll go into my office, Augusta," said Mr. Thistle in a voice like rustling paper.

The glop from the meatballs was oozing over the edge of the plate onto my hands.

It's not that I wished Karen any bad luck, but I really missed her. Her dad did her a favor when he made her stay home. How come my dad didn't do me favors like that?

And what about Mom? If she were around, this business never would have happened. Was she going to stay in California forever? I tried to remember what she looked like, but she was a blob in my mind.

In Mr. Thistle's office were a window, a coatrack, two chairs, and a very neat desk. On the desk was a picture of a much younger Rupert, like some cherub sitting on the lap of a round-faced woman who must be his mother. He looked lonesome.

Mr. Thistle pointed to a chair. "Sit down, Augusta."

I sat.

Out of the window, I could see that the rain had stopped. On Sycamore Street, a truck from the Mac-Iver Glass Manufacturing Company was bouncing past. At the Sturgis Supermarket parking lot across the street, people were buzzing into the store, and out, with grocery sacks. Food. They were going home to eat up all that food, and I was hollow inside.

My stomach growled. I could starve to death, and no one seemed to care.

Mr. Thistle took the chair behind the desk, while I sneaked a meatball into my mouth. He shifted two piles of papers into one. He divided them into two piles. He turned a paper over and read what was on the back of it. He took off his glasses and tapped them on the desk. He cleared his throat. He leaned forward. "What do you have to say for yourself, Augusta?"

"Is it all right if I eat the food, Mr. Thistle?"

Mr. Thistle erupted. "No, it's not all right." He spit the words out like flying rocks. "Dump it in here."

He picked up the wastebasket and almost threw it at me. I parted with the drippy snacks, wiping my hands on my shorts. My mouth felt like some desert, dry and forlorn.

"Now," said Mr. Thistle, "why did you do it?"

Maybe I should have told him about Pug and Karen and Miss Concannon. Only none of that stuff would make sense to him. I checked out his wiggly Adam's apple and his corncob nose and his nearsighted eyes that didn't seem nearsighted any more. "I don't know why, Mr. Thistle."

"Augusta, you don't seem to understand that this is a serious matter. Very serious. The food in Cactus Corner is reserved for customers. Anyone else who takes it is stealing."

Stealing.

I could have sworn he was looking straight into my

brain. "I never dreamed it was actually stealing, Mr. Thistle."

"I understand Gina warned you and your friend more than once, Augusta. So why did you keep coming back?"

"Well, see, the food was right there for anybody to take, so I thought anybody could take it."

"You must have food at home. I imagine your father can afford to provide for you."

I wasn't so sure it was a good thing that he knew Dad through the Chamber of Commerce. "Oh, he can provide all right. Only my mom's out of town, and Dad's extra busy, so my brother and I are kind of underfed."

"Underfed? You mean there's not enough food in the house?"

"Well, there's not all that much."

Those custardy eyes of his were clamped into position. All of a sudden there was a terrible weight in my stomach, as if I'd swallowed a hammer and a box of nails. "Well, um, I guess maybe, um, there's enough food." My voice came out very, very small.

"I should think there would be enough. I see no explanation for your coming here. We have enough problems without having to put up with childish antics."

Childish antics.

He was looking fuzzy. I was seeing him through a layer of water.

I absolutely could not let myself cry.

A tear broke loose and slipped down my cheek. I yanked my T-shirt up and wiped it away.

Would he call in a reporter? Would they print my picture in the *Bramble City Bugle* with the headline GUSSIE MACIVER CAUGHT DIPPING INTO CHEESE DIP? Would I be disowned by my parents, and by all the other MacIvers, especially Pug?

"Mr. Thistle," I wailed.

"Yes, Augusta."

"Would you please, please call my dad?"

I even gave him the phone number.

# 10.

# Really, Gussie!

Four phone calls in one day. Dad couldn't help but be furious this time.

As he walked into Mr. Thistle's office, he had a stunned look, as if he'd been banged over the head with something big. With lumps on it.

Also, he was frowning.

"Really, Gussie, this is too much! I thought I could count on you not to cause any more trouble, but my phone's been ringing all day with complaints about you. I've lost count of the calls."

"Four."

"Seemed more like forty. What's going on here, Gussie? We feed you at home, you know."

At least I finally had his attention.

"What made you do such a crazy thing?" he asked.

I couldn't answer, because all of a sudden I knew I was going to start blubbering. I needed his handkerchief. I got up and sort of staggered toward him. I was reaching for the pocket of his suit coat when—wham!—his arms came around me and he tugged me to him, hard.

Standing there with my face dug into the softness of his jacket, I felt—well, I actually felt relieved, as if I'd finally made it home after a long trip.

"Okay, Gussie, it's all right," he said, patting my back.

I nodded into his glucky lapel.

After I'd got rid of about a bathtub full of tears, he let go of me. He handed me the handkerchief, and I gave a long blast with my nose. Mr. Thistle coughed softly. "I hope you understand, Paul, that the, um, problem has come up several times."

"I'm awfully sorry, Roger. I had no idea she'd come back here. My life has been pretty hectic lately, and I'm afraid Gussie's been at loose ends."

The way they were discussing me, I could have been a piece of beef over at Sturgis's Supermarket.

"What can I do to make things right?" asked Dad.

"Don't worry about that, Paul, as long as she promises to stay away from Cactus Corner." Mr. Thistle sounded desperate.

Dad was watching me very intensely, almost as if he'd never seen me before. "Do you promise, Gussie?"

I nodded again, sniffling.

"All right. Now I want you to apologize to Mr. Thistle."

Apologize! He was overdoing it. With all the fuss, I couldn't help but be sorry for what I'd done, but enough is enough. Still, he was giving me that same steady look, with his eyebrows drawn close together. There was no way I could wiggle out of this mess. I suppose Abraham Lincoln would have been able to handle the situation easily, but my vocal cords were tied in very tight knots.

I wiped my nose and examined Mr. Thistle's tie. It was blue, with little gray polkadots. I cleared my throat. "I'm sorry I did it, Mr. Thistle. Honestly."

Mr. Thistle removed his glasses. "All right, Augusta. In that case we'll keep the entire matter quiet, although I must say—" He squinted at me, shaking his head.

"It was awfully good food, Mr. Thistle."

"Why, thank you, Augusta."

"Especially the meatballs."

Was that a smile flickering across his face?

Very quickly he shoved his glasses back on and turned to Dad. "As a matter of fact, Paul, I could use some help with my accounting here at the inn. Would you be able to straighten out the books?"

"I should think so, Roger. Be glad to take a look."

"I'll call you."

As we were leaving, Mr. Thistle shook my hand.

Dad and I walked together down the hall, with me matching my steps to his. "Crum! Seems as if everything happens to me."

"Lots of times you ask for it, Gussie."

"Well, maybe I do, but I can't help myself."

"Can't you?"

Why do grown-ups always talk in questions?

In the parking lot, he laid his arm around my shoulders, gently steering me around the puddles.

Back at the house, he said to Pug, "You go on home, Pug. We'll get our own dinner tonight."

"That's all right, Uncle Paul, I'll be happy to stay."

"Thanks very much, Pug, but I'd rather you went home."

She went home.

"Change your clothes, Gussie. I want you dry."

I changed.

Dad and Tomtom and I grilled hot dogs outside and picked tomatoes off the vine. Since the back steps were still wet from the rain, we spread newspapers and sat on them to eat, while Figaro licked up our crumbs. After Tomtom clomped inside to watch TV,

Dad leaned his chin on his hand and listened while I propped myself against the railing and told him about Karen and Mrs. Pratt and Mr. Thistle and Rupert and Beth Balenger and Diane Dunn and Meg Melvin and Mrs. Concannon and the books. He smiled and frowned in the right places. "So if you've got to have money for those messed-up books," he said, "I'd better fork over your back allowance, huh?"

He reached into his wallet and gave me the money, all of it, and I thanked him.

We watched the sun slide down behind the maple tree, tinting the clouds. We didn't say much. There was only the sound of the birds chirping away.

"Say, Dad, you wouldn't tell the relatives about, um, what happened today, would you?"

"But you know they'd understand. They're all so fond of you, Gussie."

"Maybe. Only I wish you wouldn't tell them."

"All right. If you'd rather I didn't, I won't. It's partly my fault anyway. After all, you did try to get me to listen. So I'll tell Mom when I call, but nobody else." He smiled.

Actually he's got a pretty nice smile.

Somehow I didn't mind his telling Mom. She'd be upset with me at first, but she'd come around. She always does.

After Dad had called her, I called Karen. "Gussie, for pete's sake, where are my books? I've been so bored I wrote pages and pages in my diary."

"Karen, listen—"

"I'm into December already."

"It was the rain, Karen. How could I bring your books in the rain?"

"You took the others back in the rain."

"I know, but—"

"You had the plastic bag."

Naturally she wormed the whole horrible story out of me. "But if you tell one word of this, Karen Pratt, I'll tell Sherer the Terror you're nearsighted and have to sit in the front row."

"Okay, okay. My lips are glued shut."

"I'll get your books tomorrow."

"Good."

"If it doesn't rain."

The next morning the sun was shining, and I walked with Dad as far as his office. "Aren't you awfully busy with the Platner accounts? I mean, can you really do that work for Mr. Thistle?"

"I think so. I'll have to tackle his problem, along with some others, as soon as I finish the Platner balance sheet." He gave me a sideways smile. "That is, if I don't keep getting interrupted with phone calls about my daughter."

"Well, yeah, I'm sorry about that."

"You do understand why I can't spend more time at home, don't you, Gussie?"

"Sure. Only I did sort of wonder if maybe you could possibly get to our game this Saturday. It's our last one."

"Well, if it's your last one, it comes first. I'll make it, and I'll treat you and Karen to lunch, win or lose."

I giggled. "Anything to get away from Pug."

"She means well, Gussie. After all, she came to our rescue when we needed help. The place was like the city dump before she came. Remember?"

"Uh-huh."

"So we owe her a lot, right?"

"Sure, Dad."

I was on my way home from the library when Rupert Thistle came bouncing out of the drugstore with an armful of comic books. He tossed me an enormous grin. "Well, if it isn't—"

"Rupert Thistle, you are a complete and absolute stinker."

He stared at me with his bubble eyes. His chin quivered. "Hey, Gussie, what'd I do?"

"You know perfectly well what you did. You squealed on me."

"You mean you think I— You mean that on account of that business at the motor inn—"

"That's absolutely what I think. You don't need to deny it, because I know."

"How could you know when I didn't do it? Gussie, I was at the library the whole time, and I can prove it. Listen, I didn't find out about what happened till Dad told me that she—"

"She? You mean Gina?"

"Oops! I didn't mean to say that. But somebody had to let my dad know and he'd told her to call him if you came back and she could've been fired if she hadn't and anyway you were pretty obnoxious you have to agree because you'd been warned and warned and anyway I'd never squeal on you Gussie you know I wouldn't."

He'd huffed out the entire sentence in one breath. His face was bright orange.

"Rupert," I said, "would you like to stop in at Ozzie's for a hamburger? My treat."

# 11.

# Under the Tent

If I'd known the size of Rupert's appetite, I never would have made that offer. I ended up having to fork out nearly all the money I had left to Ozzie, but I guess it sort of made up for what I'd been doing to Rupert's dad.

A few evenings later, I drifted outside to help Dad in his garden. "Say, Dad, can't we do something about Pug?"

"Honey, she's leaving for college right after Labor Day. How about hanging in there for another week?"

Labor Day. School was starting the day after. Crum! I'd be going straight from Pug to Sherer the Terror with no chance to come up for air. "Look, Dad, could you at the very least tell Pug to lay off of me? She's always bossing me around."

He turned from straightening a stake for a tomato plant to give me a grin. "I'll tell her."

When he came inside, Pug was still puttering around the kitchen, probably setting the table for breakfast. Since I was in the living room, I could easily hear what he said. He actually surprised me with his firmness. When Pug told him I was still a child, he said "Yes, but she's not a baby, Pug. She's got a whole lot of sense, you know. We can trust her to take care of herself."

So he trusted me. Even after the business at Cactus Corner. I guess he figured I'd learned something. And somehow I knew I could trust him too. Except for Mom, he'd never speak to anybody about me and Mr. Thistle.

Even so, I had to keep right on reminding him about my allowance every Friday. I guess you can't expect a parent to be perfect all at once. These things take time.

Naturally there was another big family picnic scheduled for Labor Day, for which Uncle Mac had gone all out and hired a bagpiper from the Bramble City Scots Band. That morning it was hot, and pouring rain again, but Aunt Kit called and said hi ho, and that we should come anyway, and to be sure to remember to bring the lemonade. At the last minute she'd found someone who could put up a tent. "It's a teeny bit leaky, so wear your rain gear," she said in her sheep-calling voice.

Tomtom, who had on a clean T-shirt that said HERE I AM, YOU LUCKIES, insisted on making the lemonade, and putting in too much water to fill Mom's big thermos. After we parked in front of Aunt Kit and Uncle Mac's place, he lugged the thermos out of the station wagon, tripped and fell over it on the wet driveway, and skinned both knees.

The tent was about as big as home plate. There were three eating tables at the far end, and the relatives, in raincoats and windbreakers, were wedged in around a puddle next to the drink table at the near end. Aunt Kit looked like Smokey the Bear in her wide, spinach-green rain hat, plus a matching raincoat and rubber boots. "They didn't have any large tents left," she sang, beaming out over the eating tables and chairs, so close together I didn't see how we'd be able to breathe. "We're going to be awfully cozy. Isn't that nice?"

Dad nodded, while checking out the splashes of dripping water making puddles in the grass. The tent must have been left over from the Civil War, but it didn't seem to bother Dad, who shook his head and smiled. For some reason he was almost bouncy today, as if maybe he had a secret somewhere inside him. "Where's Mother?" he asked Aunt Kit.

Aunt Kit glanced around. "Oh, fudge! She was up in her room putting on her sandals the last time I saw her. I was sure she'd be out here by now."

"I'll go see," said Dad, disappearing.

Aunt Kit turned to Corky, who had on a yellow windbreaker that looked perfect with her blond hair. I'll bet she'd look perfect in a bedspread. "Corky," said Aunt Kit, "you and Forrest will remember to pass the cake later on, won't you, dear?"

Forrest must have been the very muscular boy standing so close to Corky you couldn't see daylight between them. He didn't look familiar. "Wonder who the beefcake type is," I said to Tomtom, who was dabbing gin onto his scraped knees with a paper napkin to kill the germs.

He winced. "Ooch! He's the lifeguard at the pool, dummy. Ooch! Corky's been practically living over there all summer."

"How come you didn't tell me?"

"You didn't ask."

Before I could strangle him, Mule turned up and handed me a root beer. "Hey, Gussie, let's go inside and play video games."

On the back steps, Dad was opening up an umbrella for Grandma, who had on her pearls. "Don't be silly, Paul, I don't need an umbrella." She stabbed at it with her fist.

Dad pulled it away. "Mother, it's raining."

"Not that hard."

I cut in. "Hi there, Grandma."

"Why, hello there, um—"

"I'm Gussie, Grandma."

"You didn't need to tell me. I knew."

"Sure, Grandma."

By this time Dad had the umbrella up. He took her arm with a little bow. "Shall we?"

Grandma winked at him and took his arm, and they started downstairs.

In the den off the front hall, Mule and I walked in on a bald man in orange-and-white striped underpants, with his chest slopping over them. "Hello," said the man cheerfully. "I'm Popovich, the piper."

Mule swallowed, nodded, and shut the door fast.

I'd caught a glimpse of a plaid kilt on a chair. Somebody once told me that bagpipers don't wear anything under their kilts, but maybe Mr. Popovich hadn't heard. After a while, he popped out with the kilt on, along with a bowtie, bagpipes, tasseled socks that came up to his bulgy knees, and buckles on his shoes. "Pip pip," said Mr. Popovich, toddling toward the back door. A minute later we heard the sound

of the pipes, wailing like some cat that might have
got mixed up with a possum.

By the time the food was laid out on the drink
table, the puddles under the tent were small lakes,
and my gym shoes were sopping, as usual. The sound
coming out of Mr. Popovich's bagpipes was scratch-
ier than ever. His sweaty face matched the red wine
in the half empty bottle he had next to him on the
drink table. In all the heat, he must have been thirsty.

Mule and I started to heap our plates. Pug, who
was way ahead of us in line, looked back and called
out, "Gussie, do you realize you're right in the middle of that puddle?"

Sure enough, I was in the deepest part, with water
seeping into my shoes. So what? They'd already got
soaking wet. So why did she have to broadcast all
about my wet feet as if they belonged on the six
o'clock news?

Everybody was looking at me.

I could barely keep from throwing my plate at
Pug's face, potato salad and all.

Dad's voice came from behind me. "It's all right,
Gussie. You can take off your shoes at the table."

"Yes, of course," said Aunt Kit. "Pug dear, please
try to remember that this isn't Camp Joy."

Everyone laughed, while Pug shrugged and looked
disgusted.

Mule and I filled paper cups with lemonade and squeezed into places along the side of the tent. Somebody had put a saucepan on the table to catch a leak.

"Quiet, everybody!" shouted Uncle Mac, mopping his forehead. Mr. Popovich quit playing, and everybody shut up.

"A toast," said Uncle Mac. "A toast to all our young people who'll soon be starting school."

I really needed that toast. I picked up my lemonade and drank. It actually tasted okay. A little weak, but okay.

"A toast to all the MacIvers, whether they're starting school or not," called out Aunt Kit.

"And whether they're wet or dry," added Uncle Stew.

The lemonade tasted even better. Then, for some goofy reason, I thought about Mom. Was she wet or dry?

I pulled off my shoes and dumped them under the table. While I was eating, rainwater splashed out of the saucepan into my tossed salad, and my paper plate started to disintegrate. Grandma, next to Dad at the grown-ups' table, hollered that this party reminded her of the time she swam in the Pacific Ocean when she was six, or was it sixteen? Dad chuckled and yelled back that she might be swimming again any minute.

After Mule and I had disposed of about half our food, Forrest and Corky wriggled out of their chairs at the end of our table and made for the house to get the cake. Meanwhile, Mr. Popovich's music was sounding more and more like a cat in trouble. It had strange trills and slides to it, and finally it stopped completely. We all watched while he slowly slipped down the corner tent pole, leaving his empty glass and wine bottle on the table. He ended up in a heap in the corner with his orange-and-white underpants peeking out from under his kilt.

"Poor Mr. Popovich," somebody said.

"Can't understand it," said Uncle Mac. "They said he was their top bagpiper."

"Well, he did do his best, Mac," said Aunt Kit, "and in this awful heat."

We passed what was left of our empty plates to the end of the table and waited for Corky and Forrest to bring the cake. We waited and waited. The table and the grass under our feet got puddlier and puddlier. Grandma sneezed, while her pearls flew up and down, and Dad lent her his handkerchief. Mule and I named everybody we'd hated from kindergarten on up.

Finally Aunt Kit yodeled over to Mule, "Samuel dear, will you and Gussie take the plates out and see what's happened to the dessert?"

We sucked in our breath, inched our chairs back, and wriggled our way into some space. Corky and Forrest and the cake weren't in the kitchen, so where were they? We checked the downstairs den, where Mr. Popovich's pants were draped over the back of the sofa. We searched the whole house. We even opened a dusty trunk in the attic storeroom that was full of Grandma's old hats.

"Maybe those kids eloped," said Mule.

"Nobody ever elopes in the rain. Hey, there's one other place. The basement."

We ripped down the three flights of stairs to the laundry room. The cake was on top of the dryer, and backed against the washtubs was Corky, being passionately kissed by Forrest, with his muscular arms wound around her.

"Just like the movies," said Mule, "huh, Gussie?"

Forrest dropped his arms and stepped backward, but Corky only smiled her caramel smile. "We left the cake down here to keep it cool, and then we sort of, um, got distracted."

By the time Mule and I had helped dish out the cake and pass it around, Mr. Popovich's snoring was like rolling drums accompanying the cheery chatter around us, proving that the MacIvers always enjoy each other, even in puddles.

"Quiet, everybody!" It was Dad's voice, loud and

clear. He was standing up, with water bouncing off his right ear and no room to move.

Except for Mr. Popovich's snoring, there was silence, while everyone looked surprised.

Dad threw his shoulders back, making himself taller than ever. "In case anybody was wondering, Gussie and Tomtom and I really do appreciate the way Pug and the rest of you have kept on remembering us for the last few weeks. Maybe we're not very good at showing how we feel, but your being around does mean a lot to us. So here's to all of you."

"To us!" "Hear, hear!" "Hurray for Paul!"

I drained the last of my lemonade. It tasted terrific.

After the out-of-town relatives left, the rest of us waded inside with our empty plates and cups, leaving Mr. Popovich to sleep it off. As we filed into the house, I had a sort of queasy feeling that something was missing. What was it?

Tomtom and Uncle Stew's kids grabbed the den, so Mule and I left our shoes in the kitchen and took over a corner of the living room, where Grandma was parked in the middle of a straight chair. "My feet are wet," she yelled. "I want Paul to get my slippers."

I hadn't seen him come inside. So that was what was missing. It was Dad.

"I'll see if I can find him, Grandma."

I was spending an awful lot of time searching for missing persons.

Dad wasn't in the downstairs bathroom, and he wasn't out in the tent, where Mr. Popovich's kilt and underpants were now slightly muddy. Dad wasn't in the kitchen, in which Corky and Forrest were watching Pug put away leftover food. And he wasn't in the den, which was full of young children and Mr. Popovich's pants.

Out on the porch, the aunts and uncles were discussing what to do about Mr. Popovich.

"Excuse me," I said, "but has anybody seen Dad?"

"Why, no," said Aunt Kit. We were wondering where he was. Someone ought to call Mrs. Popovich, and Paul is always so tactful."

"And Stew and I have got to talk over some figures with him," said Uncle Mac.

I glanced into the street. Our station wagon was missing. "Our car's gone."

They all looked at each other.

"Disappeared, huh?" said Uncle Stew, screwing up his wigwam eyebrows.

"Hm," said Uncle Mac. "I'm surprised he went off without saying anything."

"Oh dear," said Aunt Kit. "Gussie, I'm sure he'll be back before long. It isn't like Paul to disappear."

Back in the living room, I said, "He's gone, Grandma. He probably went home for dry socks. I'll get your slippers."

When I got back with the slippers, Grandma was huddled in her chair, asleep. I slid her sandals off, very carefully, and eased the slippers on.

Later on, while Grandma snored and Mule and I were discussing how we ought to handle Sherer the Terror at school, our station wagon showed up in the driveway. When Dad got out, he pulled himself up straight, throwing his shoulders back. He walked around and opened the door on the passenger side, and a dark, smiling lady got out wearing a blue raincoat. It was Mom's blue raincoat.

It was Mom!

I tore out of the living room and through the hall yelling "Tomtom, it's Mom!" I heard his footsteps racing after me out the front door and through the drizzle to Mom, who hugged me hard. "Oh, Gussie!" she said when she finally let go. "Gussie!" Her eyes were big, and almost round. I'd forgotten how round they were.

I turned to Dad. "How come you didn't tell us?"

He smoothed my wet hair. "I wanted some time alone with her, Gussie. Do you mind?"

I didn't mind. Not that much.

Mom was hugging Tomtom. When she let go, she

stepped back, laying on the old maternal inspection. "Tomtom, your knees! You must have taken an awful spill."

"Golly, Mom, you should've seen the blood."

"Do they hurt, dear?"

"Could be worse, I guess."

Dad and I looked at each other and grinned.